GALILEO GALILEI AND THE BEGINNING OF MODERN SCIENCE

CARMEL REILLY

Australia • Brazil • Japan • Korea • Mexico • Singapore • Spain • United Kingdom • United States

Galileo Galilei and the Beginning of Modern Science

Fast Forward
Gold Level 21

Text: Carmel Reilly
Editor: Cameron Macintosh
Design: Vonda Pestana
Series design: James Lowe
Production controller: Seona Galbally
Photo research: Gillian Cardinal
Audio recordings: Juliet Hill, Picture Start
Spoken by: Matthew King and Abbe Holmes

Acknowledgements
The author and publisher would like to acknowledge permission to reproduce material from the following sources: Photographs by Akg-images/Erich Lessing, p 22; Corbis/RF, p 11; Getty Images/Dorling Kindersley, p 13; Photolibrary.com/The Bridgeman Art Library, p 20/ Mary Evans, p 6/ Photo Researchers, pp 15, 18/ SPL, pp 8, 9, 11, 15, 16, 17/ Superstock, p 14; The Art Archive, cover, pp 4, 5, 7, 10, 19, 21, 23.

ISBN 978 0 17 012675 5
ISBN 978 0 17 012669 4 (set)

Cengage Learning Australia
Level 7, 80 Dorcas Street
South Melbourne, Victoria Australia 3205
Phone: 1300 790 853

Cengage Learning New Zealand
Unit 4B Rosedale Office Park
331 Rosedale Road, Albany, North Shore NZ 0632
Phone: 0800 449 725

For learning solutions, visit **cengage.com.au**

Printed in Australia by Ligare Pty Ltd
4 5 6 7 8 9 10 20 19 18 17 16

THE UNIVERSITY OF MELBOURNE

Evaluated in independent research by staff from the Department of Language, Literacy and Arts Education at the University of Melbourne.

GALILEO GALILEI
AND THE
BEGINNING OF MODERN SCIENCE
CARMEL REILLY
BETELGEUSE
RIGEL
POLLUX
ANTARES
ARCTURUS
VEGA

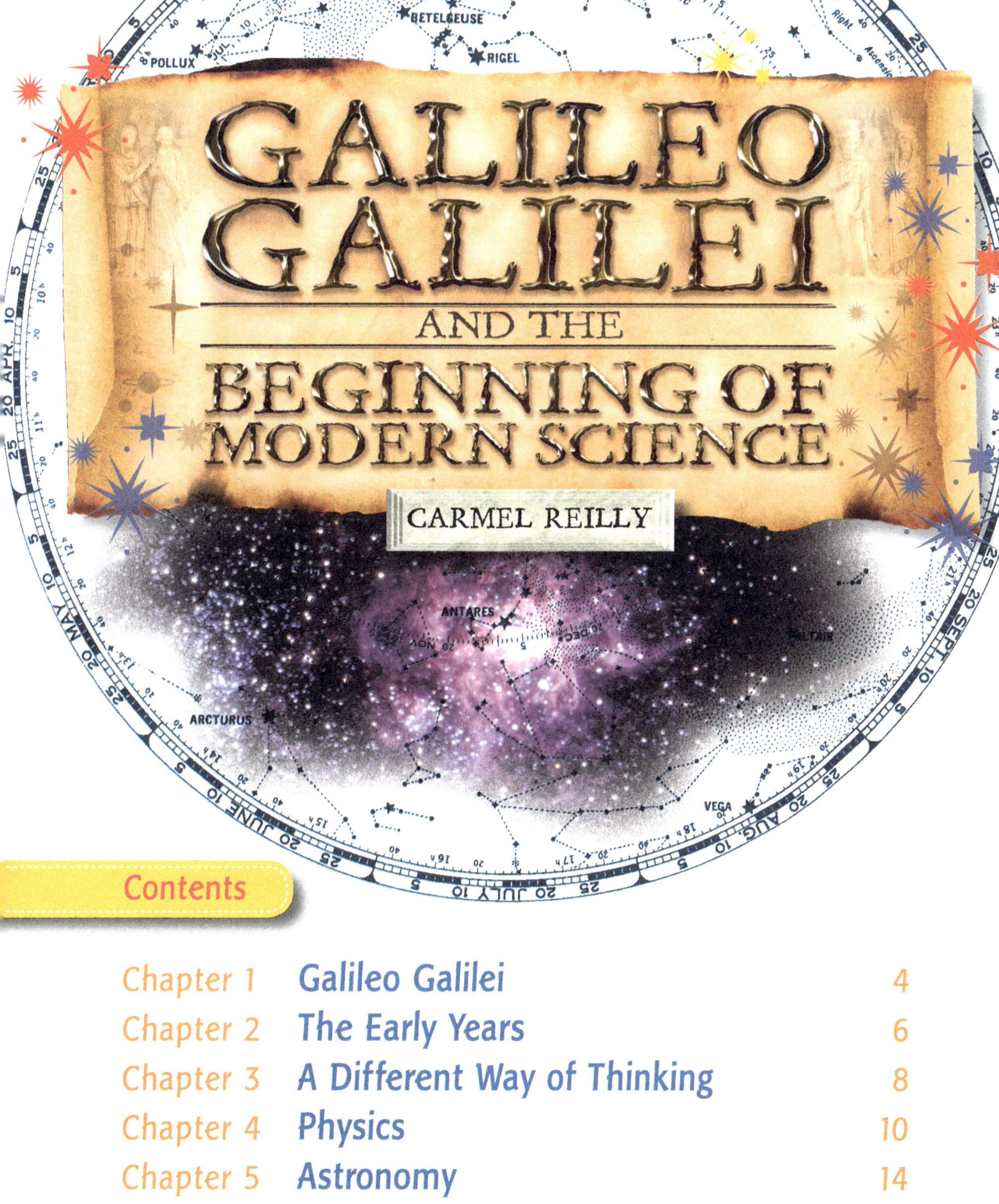

Contents

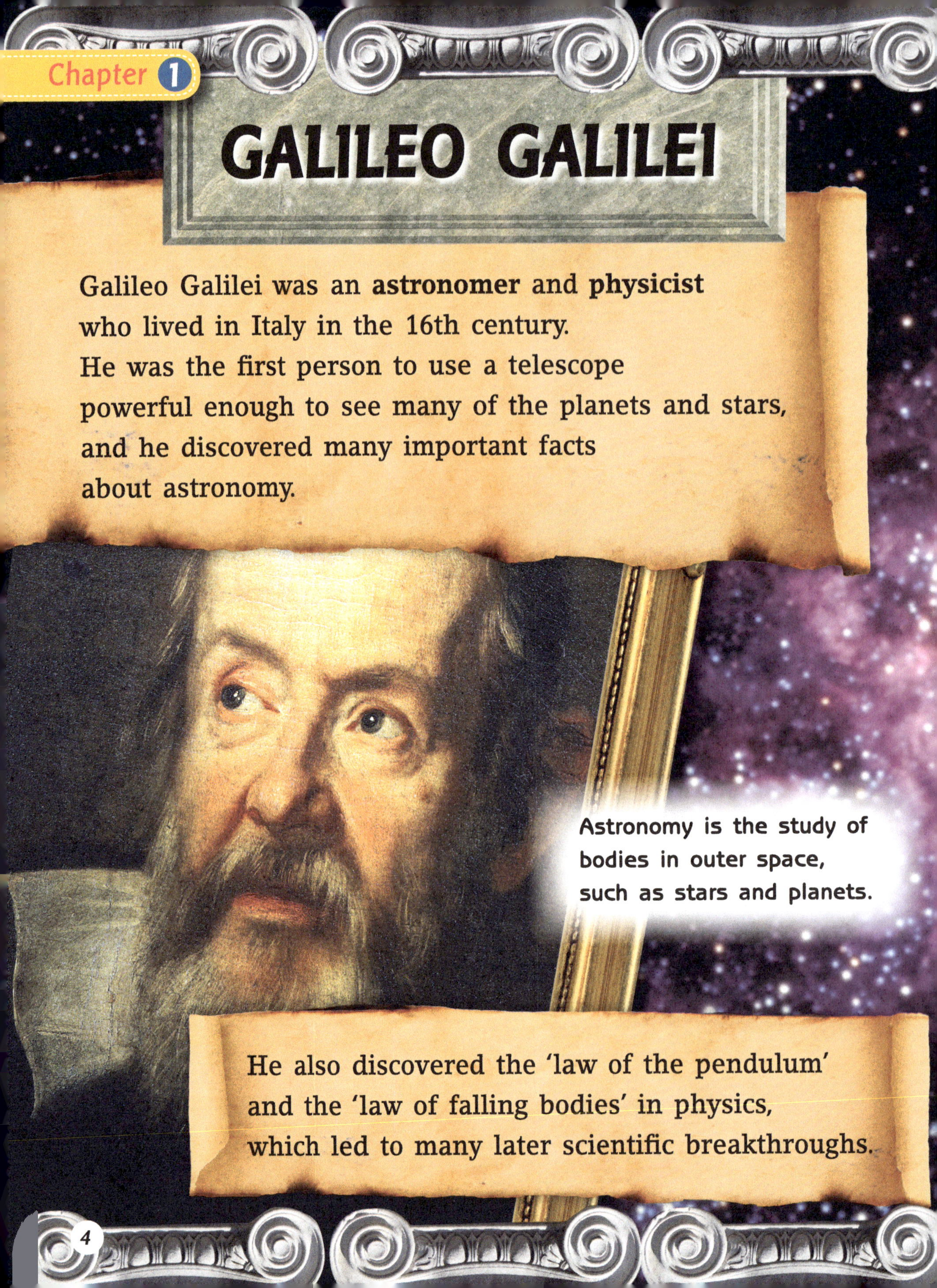

Chapter 1

GALILEO GALILEI

Galileo Galilei was an **astronomer** and **physicist** who lived in Italy in the 16th century. He was the first person to use a telescope powerful enough to see many of the planets and stars, and he discovered many important facts about astronomy.

Astronomy is the study of bodies in outer space, such as stars and planets.

He also discovered the 'law of the pendulum' and the 'law of falling bodies' in physics, which led to many later scientific breakthroughs.

Galileo is sometimes called the father of modern science, because he was one of the first people to carry out experiments and to use **observation** to find out about the world around him.

Physics is the study of matter and energy, including force and motion.

Chapter 2

THE EARLY YEARS

Galileo was born in 1564.
After finishing school, he studied medicine at the University of Pisa.
But he left after four years to become a mathematics teacher.

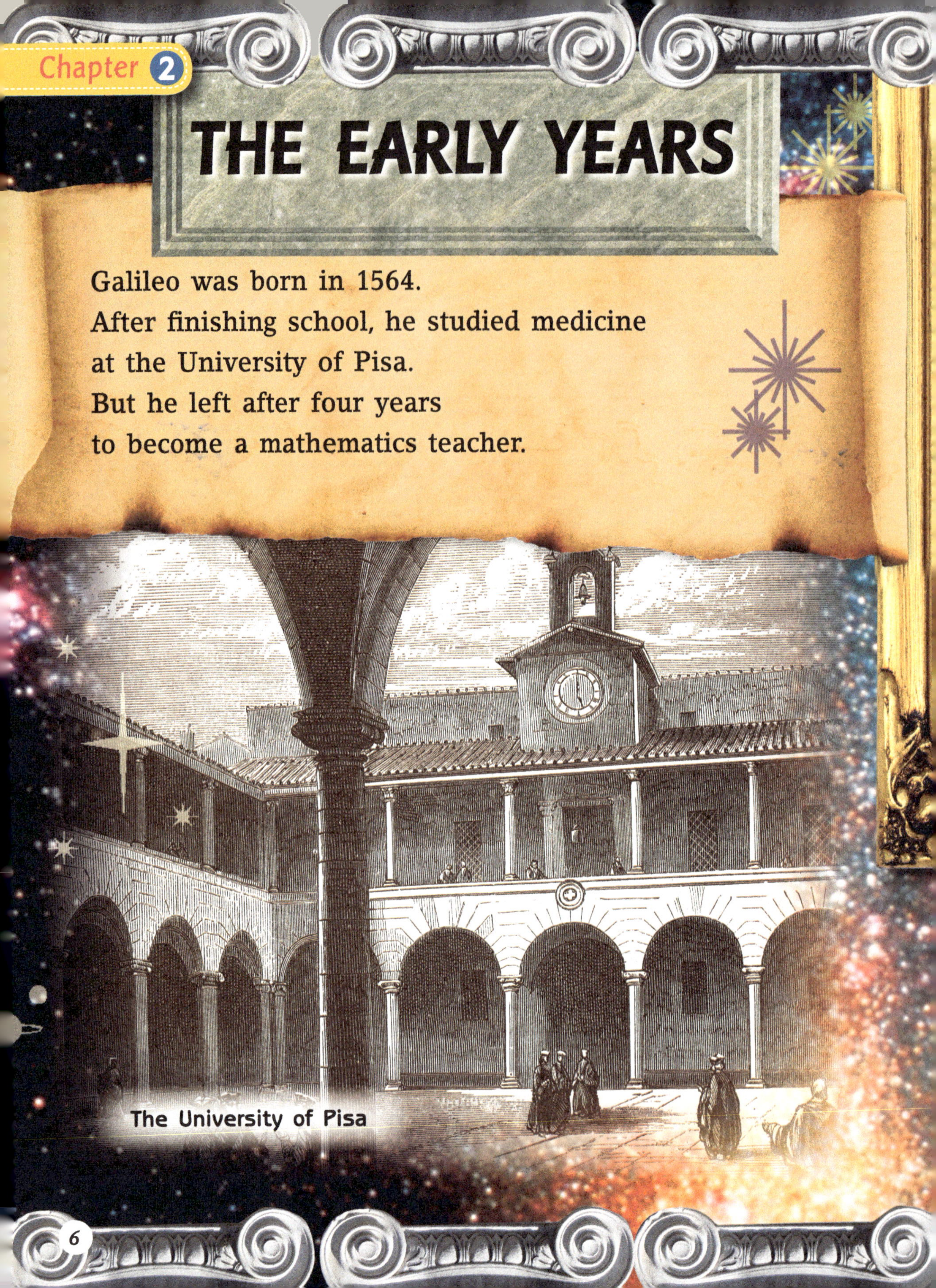

The University of Pisa

Galileo at the University of Padua

In 1589, Galileo returned to the University of Pisa to be a professor of mathematics.
Then, in 1592, he moved to the University of Padua and worked there for the next 18 years.
Throughout this time, Galileo studied astronomy and did many scientific experiments.

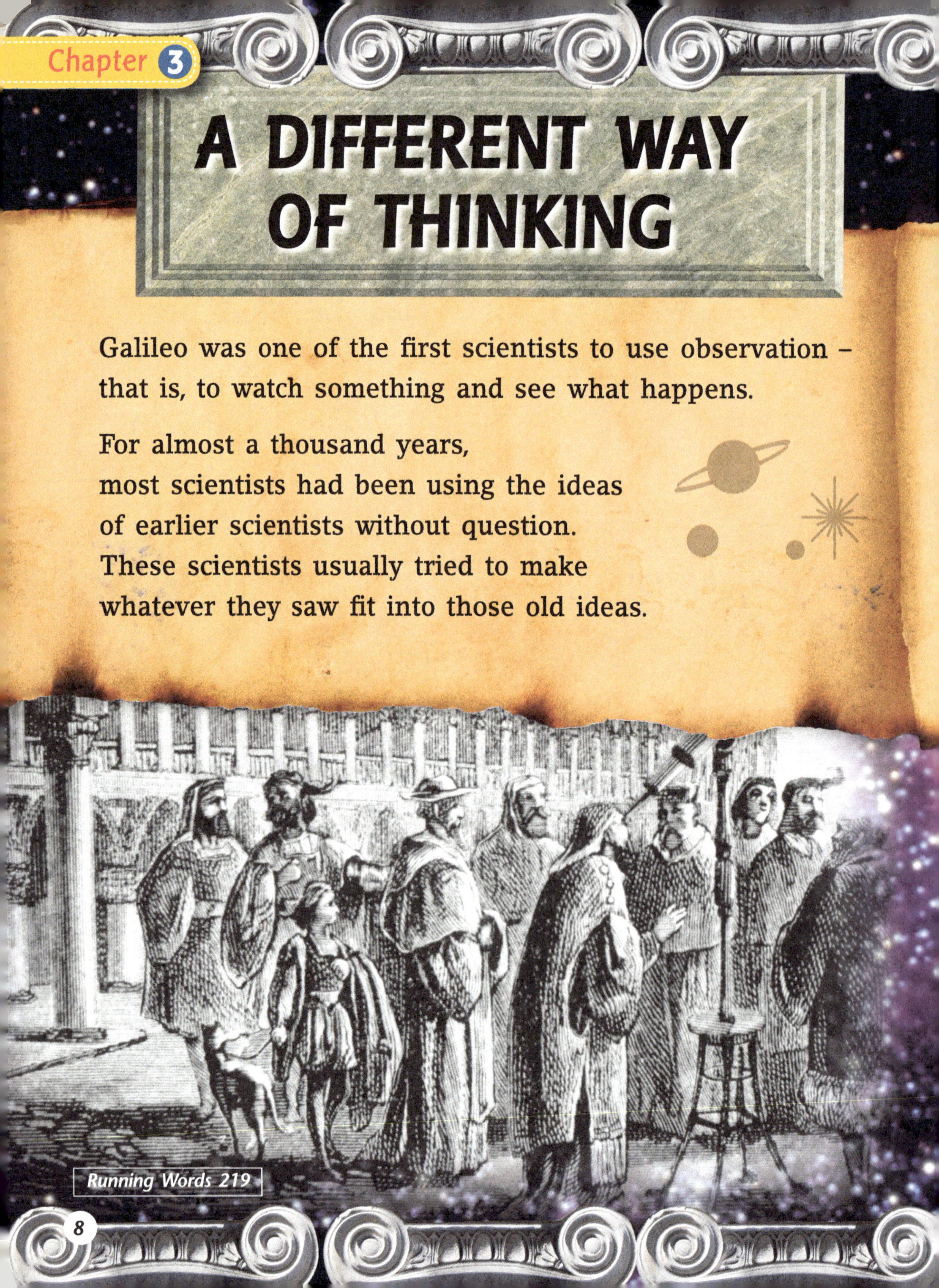

Chapter 3

A DIFFERENT WAY OF THINKING

Galileo was one of the first scientists to use observation – that is, to watch something and see what happens.

For almost a thousand years, most scientists had been using the ideas of earlier scientists without question. These scientists usually tried to make whatever they saw fit into those old ideas.

Running Words 219

By using observation and doing his own experiments, Galileo made many important discoveries in both astronomy and physics.

Chapter 4

PHYSICS

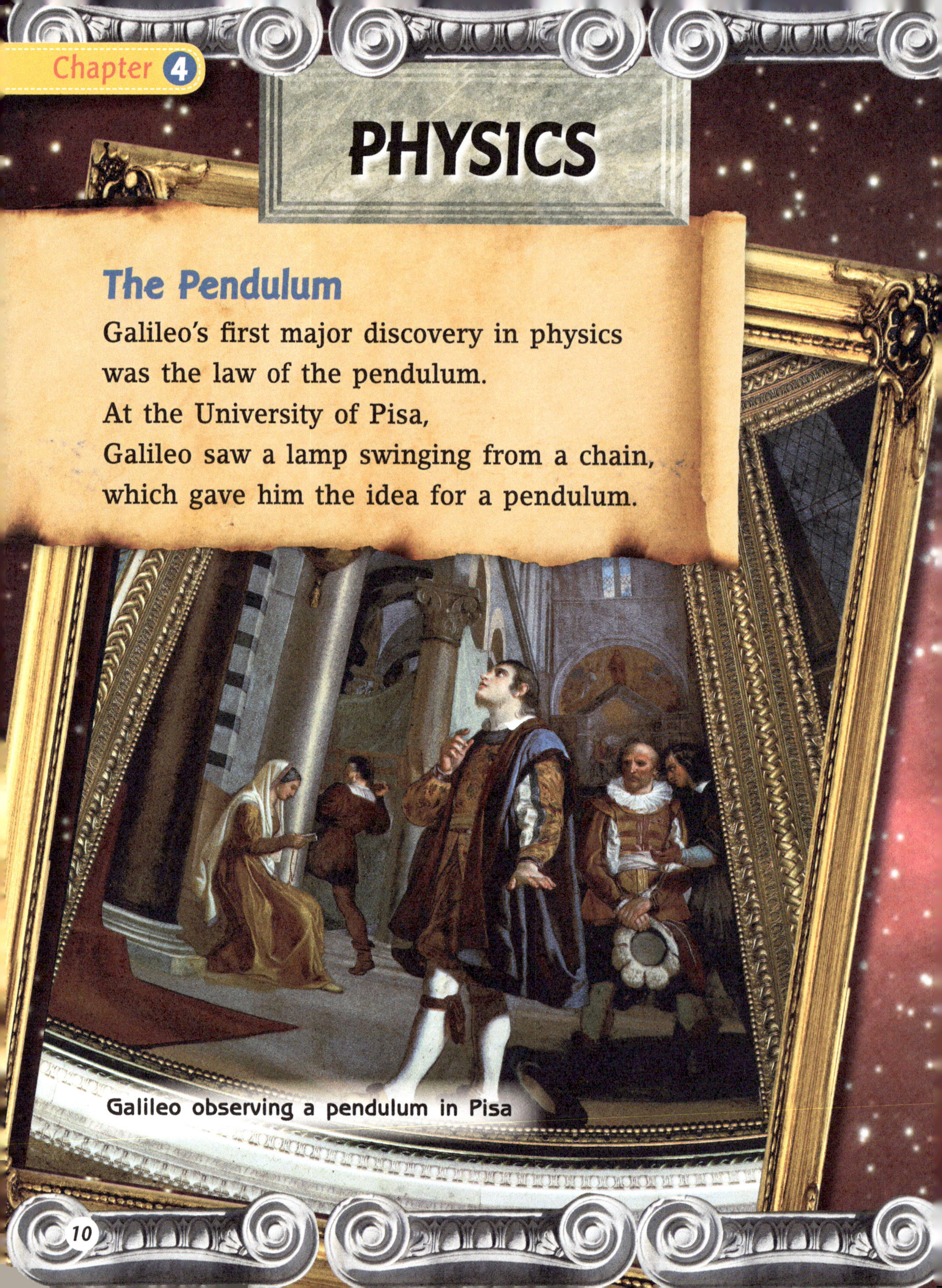

The Pendulum

Galileo's first major discovery in physics was the law of the pendulum.
At the University of Pisa,
Galileo saw a lamp swinging from a chain, which gave him the idea for a pendulum.

Galileo observing a pendulum in Pisa

After experimenting with his own pendulums, he observed that it always took the same time for pendulums of equal length to swing back and forward, no matter how far out they swung.

Galileo's pendulum clock

This discovery led to the invention of the pendulum clock – the first accurate way of keeping time.

Falling Bodies

Before Galileo's time, people thought that light things fell more slowly than heavy things. However, Galileo discovered that in the right conditions, light and heavy things fall at the same rate.

Many people believe that Galileo experimented with falling bodies by dropping things from the top of the Leaning Tower of Pisa.

the Leaning Tower of Pisa

However, it is more likely that he spent many hours rolling numbers of heavy and light balls down a small hill, and recording what happened. Galileo's work in this area helped later scientists to understand how **motion** and **gravity** work.

Chapter 5

ASTRONOMY

In 1609, Galileo made his own telescope. Only a few other telescopes had been built before, and his telescope was by far the strongest. Using this telescope, he was able to see things in outer space that other astronomers had never been able to see.

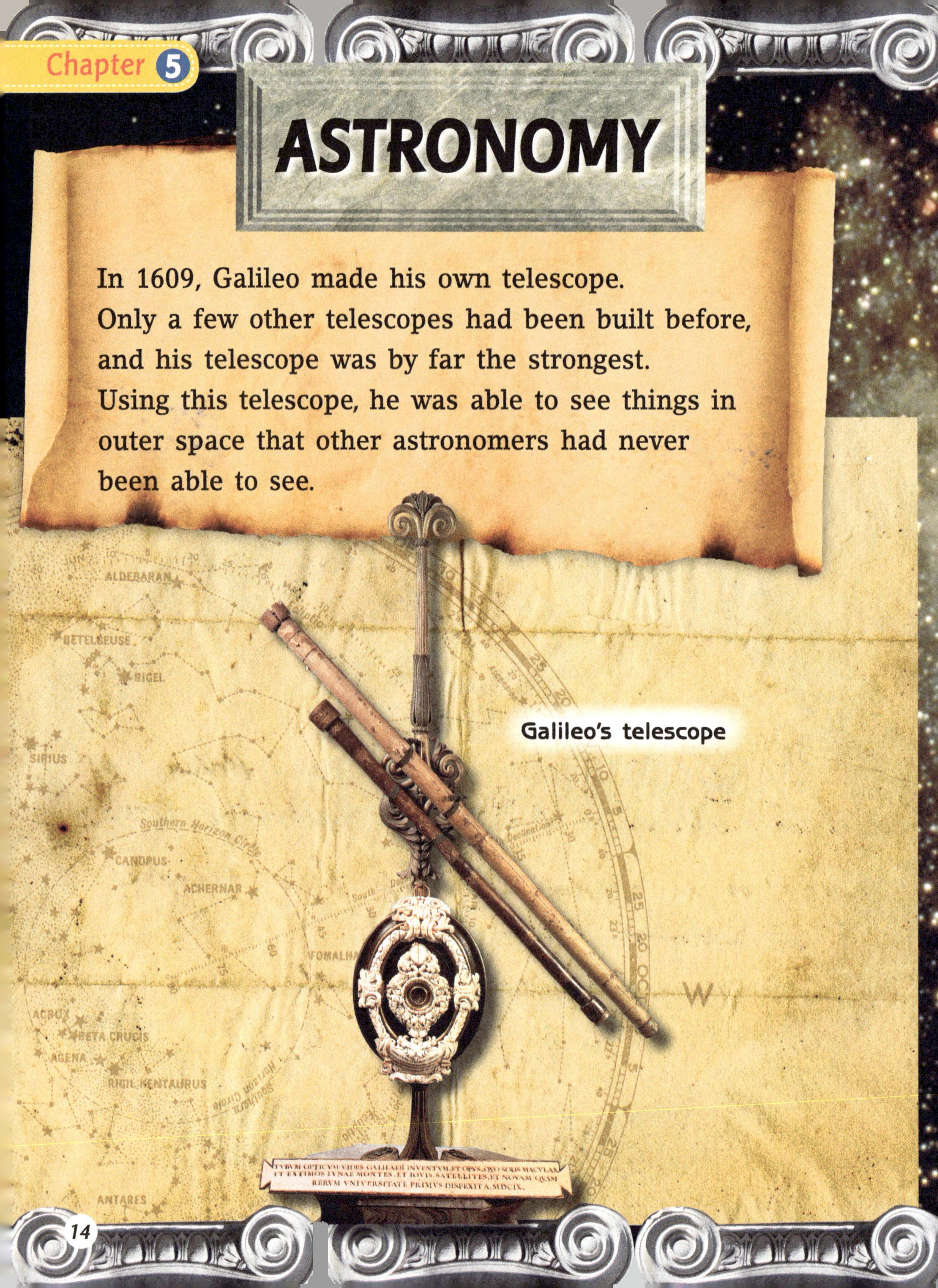

Galileo's telescope

Some of the things Galileo saw for the first time were:

- the surface of the Moon, including mountains and craters

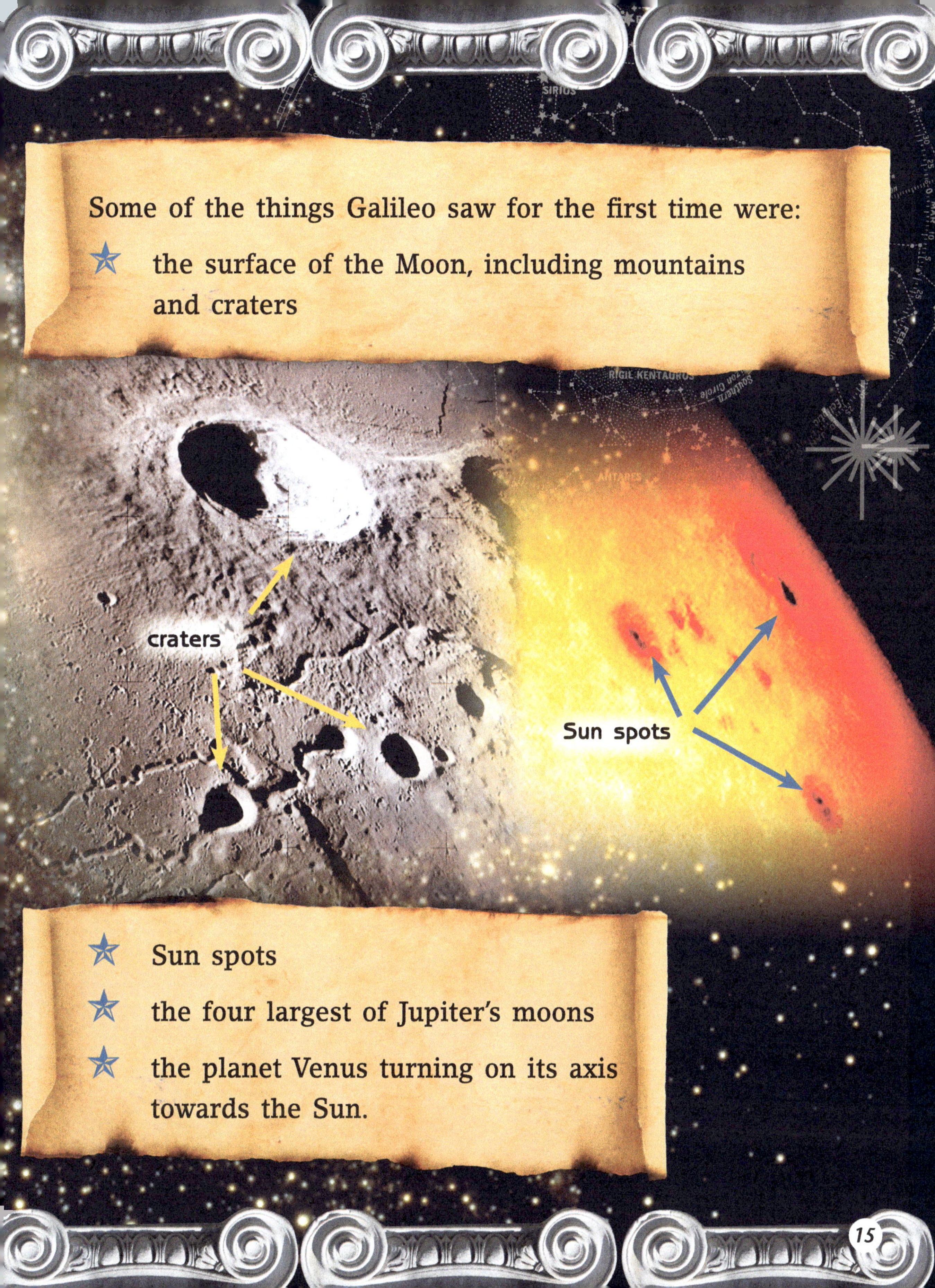

- Sun spots
- the four largest of Jupiter's moons
- the planet Venus turning on its axis towards the Sun.

Chapter 6

THE IDEAS OF COPERNICUS

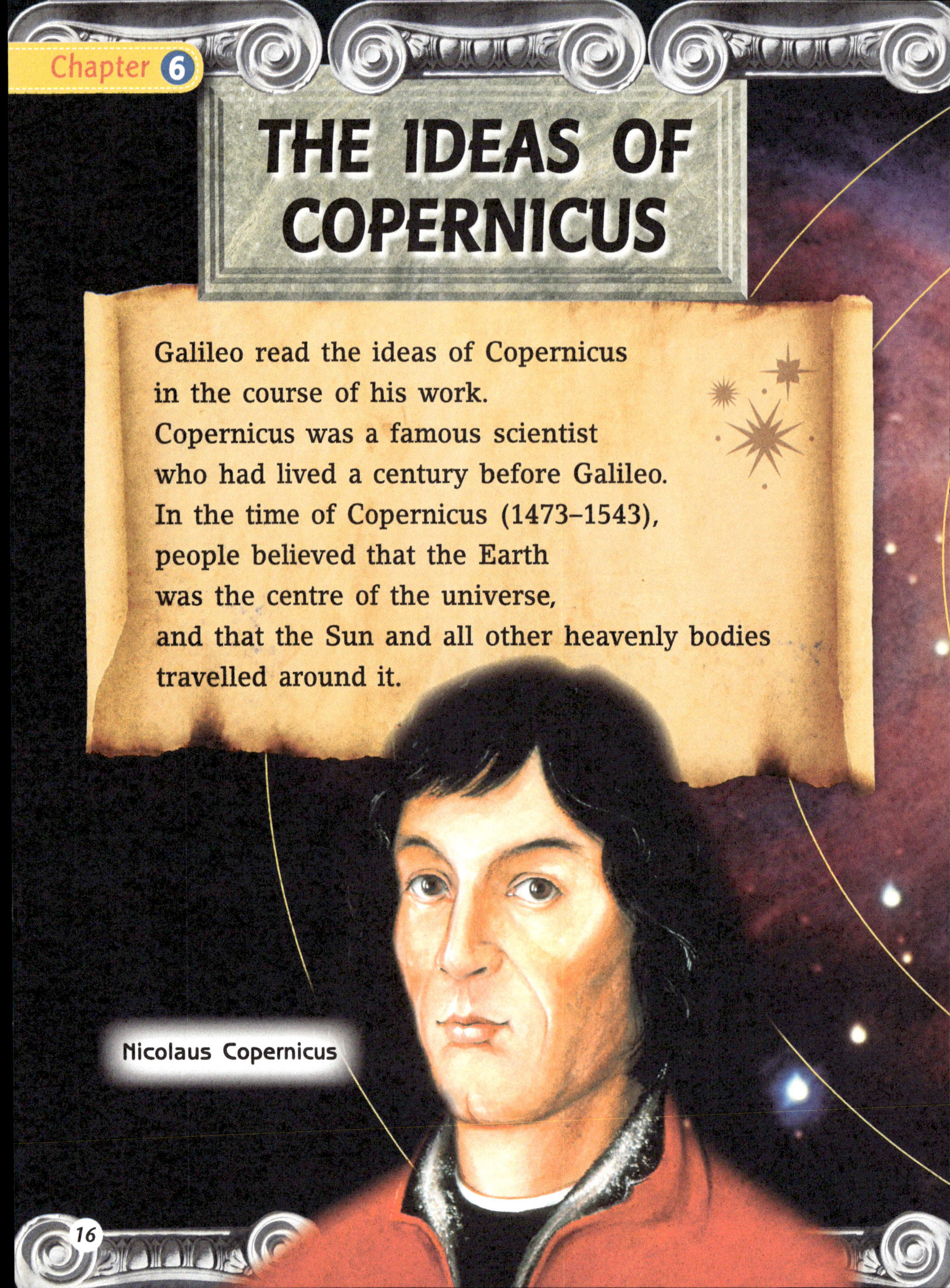

Galileo read the ideas of Copernicus in the course of his work. Copernicus was a famous scientist who had lived a century before Galileo. In the time of Copernicus (1473–1543), people believed that the Earth was the centre of the universe, and that the Sun and all other heavenly bodies travelled around it.

Nicolaus Copernicus

By using mathematics
and his own observations,
Copernicus started to think that the Earth
and some of the other planets
really travelled around the Sun.

Most people of those times could not accept
Copernicus' ideas.
It was hard for them to believe that
the Earth was not at the centre of everything.
It was also hard for Copernicus to prove scientifically
to other people that his ideas were right.

Chapter 7

GALILEO AND THE CATHOLIC CHURCH

Over time, Galileo came to agree with Copernicus' view that the Earth and other planets travelled around the Sun.
In 1610, he started to write about these ideas.

However, in Galileo's time,
the Catholic Church was very powerful,
and did not agree with his ideas at all.

Pope Urban VIII was head of the Church for the last 19 years of Galileo's life.

The Church believed that humans and the Earth were God's special creations, and therefore they had to be at the centre of the universe.
Galileo's ideas went against the Church's teachings.
To go against the Church's teachings was a crime called heresy.

In 1616, the Catholic Church tried Galileo for heresy.
He was found not guilty,
but he was ordered not to discuss his ideas again.
However, Galileo took little notice of this order.
In 1632 he put out a new book on his ideas
about the Earth's place in the heavens.
In 1633, he was tried again for heresy,
and this time he was found guilty.

Galileo's heresy trial, 1632

Galileo was put into prison
and forced to recant
(say that he had been wrong).

Chapter 8

THE LAST DAYS

Because of his age, the Church allowed Galileo to spend his last days under house arrest in the country rather than in a prison.

the room where Galileo worked in his last years

Galileo was almost blind by this time,
but he kept working
and wrote another important book
about physics.
He died in 1642.

Glossary

astronomer	a person who studies the stars and planets
gravity	the force that pulls objects towards the Earth
motion	the way things move
observation	learning about things by watching and making accurate notes about them
physicist	a person who studies matter and energy

Index